MY ADVENTURES

WITH

Disney
PIRATES of the CARIBBEAN

This book was especially written for
Captain Noah Sigel
With love from
Grandma and Grandpa

By Kate Andresen

Based on characters created for the theatrical motion picture
"Pirates of the Caribbean: The Curse of the Black Pearl"
Screen Story by Ted Elliott & Terry Rossio and Stuart Beattie and Jay Wolpert
Screenplay by Ted Elliott & Terry Rossio
and characters created for the theatrical motion pictures
"Pirates of the Caribbean: Dead Man's Chest" and "Pirates of the Caribbean: At World's End"
Written by Ted Elliott & Terry Rossio

ISBN 1 875676 21 X

Captain Noah Sigel's ship, the *Silver Mist*, was engaged in a fierce battle with another pirate ship. Things were not going well for Noah as cannons blasted holes in the *Silver Mist*. Luckily for Noah and his crew, Nico, James and Abby the *Black Pearl* arrived and fought off Noah's attackers. Noah, Nico, James and Abby were taken on board the *Black Pearl*, just before the *Silver Mist* sank beneath the waves.

'Welcome aboard the *Black Pearl*, mates! Let me introduce myself. Jack Sparrow, captain of this fine ship,' Jack called out. Noah had heard terrible stories about Jack Sparrow and his famous ship, the *Black Pearl*, but he was grateful for being rescued from the cold ocean.

'All hands on deck! Run, mates, run with the wind!' yelled Jack as the *Black Pearl* set off in search of treasure.

The *Black Pearl* had been at sea for many weeks, and they hadn't found any treasure. The crew was getting angry.

Suddenly, a crewmember yelled 'Ship ahoy!'

'Don't worry, the *Interceptor* can't catch us,' Jack said confidently. 'The *Black Pearl* is faster than any ship around.'

But soon the navy ship was right behind them. Jack had an idea. 'Head due north,' he yelled, pointing towards the dark clouds of an approaching storm.

'But, Captain,' said Noah, 'that will take us straight into the storm.'

The crew started grumbling and refused to take up their positions. Jack had to think quickly.

'Treasure! There is treasure over there,' cried Jack pointing straight ahead. Suddenly, it was all hands on deck and the *Black Pearl* caught the wind in her sails and headed straight into the storm.

The wind blew and rain beat down heavily on the wooden deck.

The *Black Pearl* skirted the edge of the storm and sailed away while the *Interceptor* was left flailing in the heavy seas.

The storm cleared and the *Black Pearl* charged through the sea with the wind at her back. Captain Jack Sparrow set a new bearing. He had to find treasure, any treasure for his crew, or he would soon be facing a mutiny!

Finally, sure that their captain was leading them to treasure, the crew settled down. But Jack felt uneasy, and with good reason! He looked astern and saw that they were in real danger! The Kraken, a huge sea monster, was closing in on them and would tear the *Black Pearl* apart if they did not outrun it.

'On deck! All hands! Run, mates, run!' yelled Jack. With a final hard pull on the ropes, they crashed into the shallow water at the edge of an island where they were safe—for now. The Kraken roared in anger.

Just then the *Flying Dutchman*, Davy Jones's ship appeared and drew up alongside the *Black Pearl*. Davy Jones was the ruler of the ocean depths and Jack Sparrow owed him his soul.

'Draw your swords, mates! Fight as if your life depends on it!' called Jack as he too drew his sword. He knew that Davy Jones would appear soon.

Noah, Nico, James and Abby drew their weapons and fought with all their strength.

'Someone needs to defend the beach,' Noah heard Jack call as he jumped from the *Black Pearl* and swam to the beach. Jack knew that Davy Jones could not step on land.

Noah, Nico, James and Abby continued fighting bravely but then Noah saw the rest of the *Pearl's* crew jump overboard and follow Jack to the beach. Confused by the crew's action, Noah instructed Nico, James and Abby to also swim ashore.

Safe on shore, a crew member told Jack, 'Jones isn't after the ship. I heard his men say that he wants to get back something that belongs to him. A three-pronged stick, he said.'

Jack sat up when he heard this. He remembered the golden trident he had found in a cave when he was a young boy. He kept it in his locker on the *Black Pearl.*

Jack decided that the only way to get rid of Davy Jones was to return the trident to him. 'Back to the ship,' he instructed his crew, but they didn't budge.

'I'll go by myself then!' he called back to them as he waded into the sea.

The crew couldn't believe that Jack was about to give up his treasure.

Back on board the *Black Pearl*, Jack went to his cabin and came out carrying a sack. As he removed the contents, Davy Jones appeared.

'I knew you would have it, Sparrow,' said Davy Jones pointing to the trident.

'Take it! But you must promise you'll leave me alone,' he said to Jones.

Davy Jones grabbed the trident and growled, 'I make no promises. Soon you'll need to pay me your debt!'

Jones and the *Flying Dutchman* disappeared under the sea.

Noah was relieved that they had gone and he called to the rest of the crew to return to the *Black Pearl*.

'Captain!' said an old sailor. 'We're proud of you for giving up your treasure!'

'I didn't give up anything. Davy Jones has taken a fancy pitchfork! This is what he was really looking for!' Jack smiled, holding up the real trident. But he knew that, one day, Davy Jones would be back.

But while Jack counted the minutes until Davy Jones would return for him, the crew of the *Black Pearl* was growing tired. They had been sailing for weeks and were desperately short of fresh food and water. With his hungry and unhappy crew, Captain Jack Sparrow set sail towards the nearest town, Port Royal.

Even though Port Royal was the headquarters of the East India Trading Company, they would have to risk the danger to stock up on supplies. In the middle of the night, the *Black Pearl* dropped anchor as close to Port Royal as she could, without being seen. The crew lowered the longboats and silently rowed towards the shore.

Life on board the *Black Pearl* was exciting but Noah was anxious to get home to Hummelstown, the rough-and-tumble pirate town where he lived. Noah, Nico, James and Abby decided to leave the *Pearl* in Port Royal. Perhaps they could find themselves a new ship?

They headed for the docks where they met Elizabeth Swann, the Governor's daughter. She told them that her father faced a big problem. Pirates attacked the supply ships that sailed between England and the Caribbean. If her father couldn't stop them, he faced being sent back to England in disgrace.

When Elizabeth heard that Noah and his crew had been sailing with Jack Sparrow, she thought that they may be able to help her father track down the *Black Pearl* and other pirate ships. Commodore Norrington recruited Noah, Nico, James and Abby and they set sail again from Port Royal.

Commodore Norrington was intent on destroying the *Black Pearl*, however, more recently, he had heard of another ship, the *Cutlass*. She had been creating fear and destruction on the high seas. Even pirate ships ran from her!

It wasn't long before the *Interceptor* met up with the *Cutlass* and Norrington instructed his crew to prepare to fight. But his crew was confused. The *Cutlass* drove pirate ships away, so why did they want to destroy her?

Norrington wouldn't listen. He didn't want any ship taking the law into its own hands. 'Raise the sails and fire when within range,' he commanded.

Cautiously, they followed the *Cutlass* as it sailed closer to the shore.

Captain Noah Sigel had not come across the *Cutlass* before and wasn't sure what to expect, especially after his recent encounter with Davy Jones and the *Flying Dutchman*.

Noah, Nico, James and Abby prepared the grappling hook as the rest of the crew drew their swords.

As the *Interceptor* drew closer to the *Cutlass*, Norrington looked through his spyglass. The ship looked empty. Then he saw someone jump overboard, swim to shore and escape through the trees. It must be the captain! 'I have never seen a captain leave his ship like that!' Norrington said.

'Quick!' said Noah as he boarded the *Cutlass*. 'Let's search the ship.' Noah, Nico, James and Abby searched the ship as Commodore Norrington went ashore with his soldiers. The captain was gone!

The *Interceptor* towed the crewless *Cutlass* back to Port Royal.

The next day Norrington told Elizabeth and Governor Swann about the missing captain. The Governor was intrigued and wanted to go aboard to inspect the ship.

Meanwhile, Elizabeth let Noah into her secret. She was the mystery captain of the *Cutlass* and she planned to rid the seas of pirate ships so that her father would not be disgraced!

During the night, Elizabeth, Noah, Nico, James and Abby sneaked aboard the *Cutlass* and set off in search of pirate ships.

That night, Port Royal awoke to the sound of cannon blasts. The *Cutlass* had returned and was engaged in a fierce battle with two pirate ships that had crept into the harbor. The *Cutlass* blasted holes through the ships and they fled, leaving the *Cutlass* alone. Elizabeth, Noah, Nico, James and Abby cheered!

Commodore Norrington ordered his men to tow the *Cutlass* into port. They boarded the ship, but found it empty again.

Norrington was angry. He didn't like being outwitted.

But Governor Swann was happy. He thought it was Norrington who had chased away the pirates. He gave Norrington a medal as a reward. Little did he know that his daughter and her mystery crew had chased away the pirate ships and saved him from disgrace.

Life in Port Royal was relatively peaceful again. Governor Swann was able to concentrate on building the trade routes between England and the Caribbean without the threat of pirate ships.

Noah was anxious to find a way back to Hummelstown. Noah, Nico, James and Abby went to the waterfront and asked the fishermen if they knew of any ships for sale. Noah thought it strange that there were so many fishermen around. Why weren't they out fishing?

When asked, one of the fishermen pointed out to sea where a ship lay at anchor. 'I am afraid of that ship,' he replied.

Nearby, Elizabeth and Will were practicing their sword fighting. Will, the apprentice blacksmith, had made her a beautiful sword and he was teaching her how to fight with it, because, as he told her, 'You never know when you might need it.'

Will and Elizabeth overheard the fisherman talking and went over to investigate.

'I won't go out to sea whilst that ship is nearby. People say it is a ghost ship,' the fisherman continued.

During his travels, Noah had heard a legend of a ghost ship but he didn't really believe it!

Noah told the others the story. 'Apparently, the ship first sailed over one hundred years ago. The captain of the ship had a special sword. Its handle had been carved with pictures of his ship and the captain's true love.

During a fierce battle, the captain lost his sword. He vowed to get it back, but before he could do anything, his ship was sunk.'

Before Noah could finish his story they heard a loud *CRAAASH*.

They looked around to see a large ship had smashed into the dock.

'It's the ghost ship causing this trouble! It's bringing us bad luck,' the fisherman called out.

'The ghost captain will not rest until he finds his sword,' another fisherman continued.

Noah, Nico, James and Abby had been at sea for a long time and had heard many stories of the ghost ship, but they had never seen any proof. Could the legend be true?

What could they do? The fishermen had to fish to support their families.

Then, Elizabeth had an idea. 'Will, can you make another sword just like the captain's?' she asked.

'I can try,' replied Will. He went to his blacksmith shop and worked all night to replicate the 'captain's sword'.

The next morning, Will proudly showed off his sword. Elizabeth was impressed. 'It's a beautiful sword, Will! Any captain would be proud to own it,' she said. 'Now, all we have to do is get it aboard the ghost ship and hope that the captain will find it.'

'We should wait until nightfall and then row out to the ghost ship,' suggested Will to the rest of the group.

In the dark of the night, Elizabeth, Will, Noah, Nico, James and Abby rowed silently out to the ghost ship. When they came alongside her, Elizabeth was first to climb up the rope ladder. Carefully, she carried the 'captain's sword'.

The others joined her on the deck and had a look around. It was very quiet apart from the sound of the waves splashing against the hull. There didn't appear to be anyone on board. It was very spooky. Noah, Nico, James and Abby went down below.